C000185211

BOTH
PUBLISHING

Published in 2021 by BOTH Publishing.

The author asserts their moral right to be identified as the author of their work, in accordance with the Copyright, Designs and Patents Act, 1988.

A CIP catalogue record of this book is available from the British Library.

ISBN - 978-1-913603-10-6
eBook available - ISBN - 978-1-913603-11-3

Printed in the UK by TJ Books Limited.
Distributed by BOTH Publishing.

Cover design by Chrissey Harrison and Alistair Sims. Typeset by Chrissey Harrison.

Part of the Dyslexic Friendly Quick Reads Series.

www.booksonthehill.co.uk

THE
BREATH

Joel Cornah

**Other dyslexic friendly quick read
titles from BOTH publishing**

The House on the Old Cliffs

Ultrasound Shadow

The Clockwork Eyeball

Anchor Point

At Midnight I Will Steal Your Soul

Sherlock Holmes and the
Four Kings of Sweden

The Man Who Would Be King

The

Breath

The Gates had collapsed over a generation ago. Finding the parts necessary to fix one had been called a waste of time. But Hala had done it.

For fifteen years, there had been silence from Wayna V. Trying to convince the Allied Councils to send a scouting ship had proved fruitless. If there was anyone there, the cloud of storming meteors made it too difficult to get to them. They had deemed it not worth the risk.

Hala had been tuning her Gate into

the frequency of this dead world for a week. A mark five was better than she had hoped for when she had been assigned the task. She had studied old rocket technology in school, but Gates were still a fascination. Her face split into a smile as she recalled being able to identify rocket pads of thirty different kinds. It had made her friends embarrassed to be around her.

Her school days seemed a million years ago – her days as a student, specifically. Being a research professor meant she was still in a school. The Terran University had indulged her expedition, on the condition she had arranged funding herself. This survey of a lost planet was of little interest to anyone but a few in the Astro-Anthropology Department. She was surrounded by people who could name all the lost planets, but none of them had ever set foot on one. Wayna V was a niche even among these academics, as information about it was scarce and dull.

Breathing apparatus stamped with the University emblem was pinned to her back while a helmet was screwed over her head. Three fellow researchers worked on her suit, fixing its pressure valves and making sure they were within easy reach.

Hala took an experimental breath, the suit's tubes and pipes filling in response, pumping air directly into her lungs. She felt groggy from the surgery that had fixed the things inside her body.

"We're not sure what to expect," said Shula, the team leader. "No readings are coming through, and the robots haven't been much use. Whatever happened, it wasn't a picnic."

"Reassuring as ever, Shula," Hala mumbled and tried to smile.

Shula had been the one who had got Hala interested in this planet. They'd met at the offices of one of the University's top donors. Waiting for rich people was a pain, and they'd shared stories of the most ridiculous hurdles they'd had to jump through.

Wayna V was an obsession for the

pair of them. Shula had excitedly told her about the indigenous life and the legends of the ghostly gods. There was brightness in Shula's eyes when she'd talked, and a crease to her forehead whenever she'd mentioned how it had all been lost.

Hala rolled her shoulders and stepped closer to the prism doorway. It was diamond-like in shape, a glass face that split the light into rainbow bands. Each colour bent back and around, forming a continuous loop of light that rolled in a bubbling cloud. Her hand was still in her friend's.

"Keep in contact," Shula said, letting go of her fingers. "You might not be able to hear us, but assume that we can hear you. If nothing else, your suit will record everything."

"I'm not a great public speaker," she said, lowering her voice.

"Don't I know it." Shula snorted. "When you gave the presentation to Monarch, they thought you were going to throw up."

Hala smiled sheepishly. The Monarchs had had relatives on the planet in question. They were the richest people for light-years. Virtually nobody could breathe the same air as them, let alone give a presentation to one of them. Not that they had been there in person; the whole thing had been recorded and sent off. Hala wasn't even sure Ms Monarch herself had seen it – probably one of her subordinates.

"I still don't get why we had to go there to record the thing." Hala frowned deeper and cracked her fingers.

"Establishing dominance." Shula shrugged. "Make everyone go to them and only accept the people who come crawling on their hands and knees."

"I'm glad they took an interest."

"I expected them not to bother. They liked you, though." She put an arm around Hala and squeezed.

Wayna V had been stagnant, that much was known. Its mines and refineries hadn't grown in decades. But there was a mark on one of the oldest files suggesting that it had had remarkably clean air. The Monarchs had sent one of their children to help grow industry on the planet. It seemed to work for a while, but then communications stopped. Investigation was too expensive, and soon the planet was lost.

The loss of their son – a fifteenth level cousin of the chief heir, but a Monarch none the less – had been what had clinched it. Fifty-five meetings, strenuous negotiations over budgets, and almost a year of paperwork. Moreover, the family had given them Beta-Nine-Z-X security clearance. Hala wasn't sure what this meant, but she had downloaded the codes into her computer just in case.

"Watch out for swarms," Shula said. "The Old Gods, they called them. I'd love to study them. Fascinating stories, you should read them."

"Mythologies and all that?"

"Yes. They say these Swarms would use old world tech to get around – pipes and steam. They talked to people, they changed things, they predicted the future. The settlers worshipped them. They disappeared, though. The myths and legends stop and then apologetics take over. Maybe they couldn't use microchips or something?"

"Or they died with the planet."

"You'd think gods would be bigger

than that. If they saw it coming, they'd have stopped it, done something. If they were as powerful as the legends say, they wouldn't just have stood aside. I suppose we'll never know."

"Lost planet, lost gods."

The Gate glowed green. Hala took a breath, squeezed Shula's hand, and stepped forward. "It's time," she said.

"Come back in one piece," Shula said.

"I will do what I can." She smiled as she took another step. Her heart thudded. It was now or never. "When I get back, we should have a drink."

"Or five," Shula agreed. "Be safe."

Light enveloped Hala, and she was dragged through knives of cold. Pain stabbed every inch, light burned; it was like being hit with bricks from the sun.

She landed on soft sand, panting and sweating as though in the throes of the worst flu. No wonder Gates had fallen out of fashion.

Rolling onto her back, she stared at the sky which roiled like lumpy soup. Her arm vibrated and she lifted it to stare at the screen built into the suit. Atmospheric conditions seemed regular and the gravity was only a little stronger than what she was used to.

Standing was a struggle, and by the time she was up, she was out of breath.

The suit's systems took a while to compensate. Dizzy, she took gulps of air while leaning on the humming machine beside her. It was the same model as back home but in much worse repair. She hadn't thought that possible given that the University had fixed theirs with string and tape.

"Shula, can you hear me?" she asked. Her com hissed white noise.

She cast her eyes about. There was a desert, red and grey in stretches. Boulders beaten by wind and the shells of shanty towns were scattered at the bottom of the hill she stood atop. Sitting on the ground, she waited for the internal bio-systems to calibrate and calm her nerves. Air filtered into her lungs through pipes embedded in her chest. She didn't need to breathe, but she did anyway; it was a habit, though she had heard that people who used these things regularly could train themselves to stop breathing altogether.

The computers in her suit analysed the surrounding areas, and while they worked, she pulled up some data Shula had stored in the banks. As the titles of various legends of the planet came up, she smiled at her friend's obsession.

Attached to one tale – a story of the gods stopping the collapse of a tower by breathing on it – was a commentary. The author wrote in long, waffling passages that wormed through the story, making airy points about life and how it related to the gods.

**'Even when all is
collapsing, the breath
remains,' they said. 'This
story teaches us to trust to
the gods, even when all is
failing around us. Believe
hard, and they shall put
their breath into us. My
friends, know that the gods
act, and we will be free.'**

Hala looked around at the ruined
town and made a face. The gods hadn't
seemed too interested in stopping
whatever caused this catastrophe, she
surmised. Sadness passed into her, and
she considered heading back through the

gate, but its power was still recharging. She was about to read another legend when something caught her eye.

Two points of light blinked from the shantytown. Her heart threw blood about her body in a calamity. The lights moved, stalking into the streets. She scrambled over the ashes and broken electronics at her feet. Her eyes went to the foaming sky; it was a war of clouds that rumbled with menace. But the dry earth suggested that it had not rained for a long time.

"I don't know if you can hear me." Her voice cracked as she spoke. She wanted to say more, but blood was rushing to her face and her throat closed.

In her mind, she saw the others listening. Would they laugh? She knew her voice wasn't the most impressive. Talking had always been a problem. Somewhere in the back of her mind, she had thought that coming alone would have been better. Nobody to intimidate or distract her. But speaking into nothingness seemed just as intimidating. The expanse of space around the shantytown was like a gaping ear, ringing with every word she spoke.

Lights shot between two hollow buildings, a clang and hiss thundering with the movements. Hala tensed, her fingers turning cold as her spine became rigid.

"I'm not alone," she said into the

com. "I think …" Words wouldn't come.

The air dispenser whispered and clicked, pumping breath into her lungs. Her hand went to the controls on her arm and she turned the oxygen up, lightening her head as it weighed her down. Striding through the shattered town, she spied bonfires long since dead. Kneeling beside one, she lifted a corner of bright yellow paper that had survived. The eye and nose of a face was visible. The high forehead and shining pupils were familiar, but not too familiar.

Hala had been fortunate to get a scholarship, bringing her out of the misty streets and into the University. Occasionally she had lent money to her family, but this was frowned upon. She hadn't cared until she'd been brought to a tribunal, accused of smuggling. Shula had helped with her defence. She was always there, always helping. Hala still felt guilty asking for anything when she'd done so much already.

The visor on her helmet flashed a warning. She turned and stumbled. A shadow was building against the building opposite, glowing eyes at its base.

"I can see it," she whispered. "It's a …"

The shape emerged, clanging and hissing steam between joints. It was a wolf, fur rising on its back and half of its face, but the rest was coated in a conglomeration of pipes and valves.

The mouth opened, revealing teeth the size of Hala's fingers.

"A mechanised wolf," Hala said.

It reared its head and steam flowed between its teeth. Hala reached a hand to her air controls, trying to make her heart slow. The wolf lifted its maw and let out a howl that shook her visor.

Hala ran, skidding through broken streets, sprinting this way and that, pushing ever faster, harder, the pain in her legs mounting until she slammed into a wall. The shock knocked her lungs into frantic pulses while her visor flickered.

Her visor pointed her left, warned

of trip hazards, and sent alarms as the wolf closed in behind. The computer struggled, mapping the shantytown and suggesting routes. She pelted down alleyways, under bridges, across a bone-dry riverbed, and finally towards a courtyard. A well gaped in its centre, broken buckets filled with sand around it.

She waited a beat, and then another. The wolf was nowhere in sight and she took a long, shuddering breath.

A wall nearby was coated in posters. They all showed the same face, but most were hidden under graffiti. There was hatred and violence in the vandalism, some posters torn down, others defaced to a blackened mess. She stood, taking in the sight of unbridled rage directed at the wall.

The face on the posters was unrecognisable. She approached, reached out, and pulled one free. It was brittle and crumbled in her glove, but she caught a glimpse of blue in one of the defaced eyes. Words had been scrawled on the poster with fury turning to desperation. The angry letters were large, jagged; there was a bite that Hala could feel just looking at them. Later pens had been small, shaken, and there was something about them that left her feeling hopeless. It took her some time, but eventually, she pried out the words.

'The gods have abandoned us. The new gods hate us. Why? Why?

Why?'

Flicking the visor's internal memory back on, Hala searched for another legend with commentary. Her curiosity pushed her, so she searched for the word 'why' and her lungs tightened when she found it. Much like the graffiti artist, the apologist repeated it over pages and pages. She felt her mouth go dry and it took the system a moment to push moisture back into it. The text was alongside the story of a wind god rescuing starving children.

> **'The people cry out, "Why have they abandoned us?" They point to our legends, to this tale, and**

they ask why we do not see these things now as they were in the tales. The answers exist, but I fear they may be too terrible to contemplate. The gods are powerful beyond our minds, but how are we to reconcile their inaction in this time of need?

'I feel the answer within my grasp and I feel it in my breath. It is a test of our faith. As we see our families fall and our buildings crumble, the gods watch and wait. We must firm up our faith and be

**like unto the breath, so
that the breath may enter
us and become us.'**

Her mind churned with images of starving families huddled around a church or a preacher, hoping to find solace. It made her chest ache until the suit soothed it for her.

Hala made her way over the stones and scrambled up to what had once been a gateway. The arches had fallen and the metal doors were bent, but she could still squeeze through.

"There's a metropolis," she said into the com. "Rusted buildings and odd mosaics. There are pipes, too. They run all around – I don't know what they're for. They go into each house."

The houses had bent, twisted beams and rust-scattered. Hala's legs regained strength, and she walked. The systems regulated her temperature, but the place made her shiver as though cold. Above, the clouds shifted, grumbling. Some houses had been barricaded, but the blockades had been overturned among scattered remains of food capsules. She picked one up; it was empty except for dust. She stepped over the threshold and followed a pipe to the centre of a room. An altar stood, built from steel and copper, valves and pressure gauges. But none of it was connected properly. Though she knew little about how gas lines worked, Hala could tell this was not how it was supposed to look.

She prodded the machine, but when it did nothing but threaten to keel over, she left it. Moving out to peer into other houses, she saw more altars. A popular religion. Or perhaps it was enforced. She didn't want to think about that.

The metropolis was endless. Hala passed streets and climbed stairs to sweeping skywalks that wound about domed roofs. She came to a tangle of mezzanines that bunched into a spaghetti of paths. Crossing from one to another, she forced her way past the confusion and came to the summit of an overlook.

"There's a tower," she said into her

com. Other words failed.

It was a staggering monolith of jet black. Just looking at it hurt her eyes. It was a thick, dark fact looming over the city. Atop it was a jagged structure, and she pressed her visor to zoom in. The metal was melted and twisted in horrific shapes tall enough to reach into the clouds.

"I think the top of it exploded." Hala's face warmed as she spoke awkwardly. "I'm going to investigate."

The silent world pressed. Hunching her shoulders, she started on her way. Street after street and road after road, rising above buildings and diving below. The lower regions were tangles of weeds and pipes in jagged patterns. The higher plains were no less disorganised, rotten papers and smashed glass coating the path and crunching underfoot.

Her heart tightened, and she flashed her eyes to the left. A face was glaring at her, unblinking and grinning. Her breath slowed as the computer adjusted and her mind settled. It was a poster; from the gaudy colours, she guessed it was the same as the ones she had seen defaced earlier.

It showed a smiling man with bright eyes, his tall forehead and widow's peak; the image bore into her head. She and Shula had been waiting at the docking bay of the Monarch palace moon. The nightmare of gold and gems that covered every conceivable surface had reportedly bankrupted three planets. The Monarchs had owned said planets and claimed a right to destroy them at their whim.

Shula was usually brash, unfiltered, and forward. But standing in the waiting area with the fate of her research project in the balance – five years of study and six of fieldwork – she was subdued.

"We require you to undergo a medical examination," the staff had told them. It had been the first time Hala had seen a reflective interface. She had been looking at her own face in the polished gold wall when her features had shifted and were replaced by the image of a young man in pink dress. "It will be a simple procedure."

"May I ask why?" Shula had said.

"Ms Monarch likes to know who she is giving money to." The holographic reflection moved, pointing them to the door, which then opened and revealed a white chamber. Shula had urged Hala to go first. The procedure had been simple; a scan from a whirring machine which hummed across her body, followed by a blood sample.

She was asked to wait while Shula was examined. Hala wasn't sure how long she had been waiting, but it felt like hours. When the staff had returned to the wall, they informed her that Shula had been sent back the University.

Hala gave her presentation, and they were given funding, but it was half of what they had asked for. They had taken it, but Hala still wondered why Shula had been shunned. When the old woman had handed over the security clearance, Hala asked about Shula, but the computers had refused to even recognise the name.

"Don't worry about it," Shula insisted when next they met. "I know what I'm doing. Besides, this gives you an opportunity."

They had not talked about it much.

"It's the face of the staff," she informed the com. "Shula, I don't know if you can hear. But it's the same face here on these posters."

She tapped her biological controls, lowering her heart rate and calming. The system that maintained her body was old, but it was more advanced than anything she could have afforded on her own. Even with the University's backing, they would never have got this far, so she shook her concerns away. It was easier to focus on her work.

'Legends aren't gods,' some graffiti said. **'To become a god, ignore the stories.'**

'Don't feed the addiction,' another proclaimed. **'Let the gods starve!'**

Hala scrutinised the words. More had

been written, but it was illegible under the years and rival scrawls. Weeds had eaten much of the warring manifestos.

Gulping, she crept from the wall and slid into a street before heading to another skywalk. It wound around a palace-like structure and above most of the other buildings. Now closer, the monolith was even starker, its blank face foreboding and harsh.

Above, the clouds were darker, a congealed mess of bulbous coral. Enhancing the view through her visor, she examined the clouds as she paused, allowing the oxygen systems to recalibrate. They had been extracting what little they could from the atmosphere and would filter it for her, but it took time.

The clouds emanated from the monolith. Unease was building, and Hala wrung her hands as the computer flicked words and numbers at her.

Steam hissed and a growl trilled through her suit. The alarms leapt to top volume, pointing her to the thing she was staring at with watering eyes. The wolf was stalking, its haunches raised and fur bristling. With a clang, it moved one paw forward, copper pipes rolling above its joints and into its body, vibrating with inner heat. Steam and mist coiled, whispering, moving unnaturally.

"The Old Gods," she whispered.

"Shula, I see them!"

She clutched at her heart, feeling the myriad tubes that fed into her bloodstream and trusting that they were feeding her body enough to keep her going.

Her oxygen tanks were straining, her legs ached, but she thundered on, pounding through streets, the shadow of the monolith deepening. In and out of streets, under skywalks and over them, she kept running, hardly daring to look back.

The face of the monolith was before her, the gutters of gold clear and glittering. Alarms screamed in her ears. The wolf was moments away, the hiss and growl coming in great gulps. She tightened a fist and ran at a door set into the otherwise blank face of the structure.

Her shoulder slammed into it and throbbed. With a heaving force of will, she pressed harder. The trilling steam escaping from valves made her tense. She risked a look. The wolf was running, clattering, and hissing. Hala pounded on the door, kicking and shouting. Her hunter was seconds away, the sound of its breath overtaking everything else that rang in her head.

It crouched mid-sprint and the joints squealed. Instinct made her duck. With a rush, the wolf soared over her, leaping with unnatural power and crashing into the door, shattering through. The monolith growled and vibrated, its face cracking. The hole where the door had been led into a dim corridor. Debris and glass were scattered over the threshold, and the wolf lay in a heap surrounded by it.

Hala stepped inside, her eyes looking past the warnings on her visor to the animal that panted on the ground. It looked at her in return and blinked as its tongue lolled out of its open mouth.

"Please present your security pass," a voice sounded from her left.

Hala jumped and stumbled against the door frame. Her chest was full of wasps, and she scanned for any sign of the owner of the voice. On the wall, she caught her reflection, but it wasn't her own body. Moving a hand, the reflection copied, but it was somebody else's arm in the image. It was an old woman this time, not the young man who had staffed the office moon. She had a pleasant smile and a small pink hat, but her clothes were almost as pale as her skin. Hala felt out of place as the woman mirrored her awkward stance.

The wolf was focussing on the woman in the mirror. Inching towards the far wall, Hala tried to step behind the creature, but it got to its feet and seemed to fill the space.

"Please remain still," the interface said with a wide grin. "Damage has been caused to the entrance." There was a slam, and the world went dark.

Hala screamed and flicked her visor to night vision. Turning to the door, her stomach lurched. Something had fallen across the exit, blocking her way. The computer told her it was solid steel, the same as the rest of the monolith.

The glowing eyes of the wolf sent shadows skittering, and Hala backed from it until she hit the blockage. Haunches raised, the creature sniffed her and bared its teeth. Blood trickled from wounds on its head, but slivers of metal were winding their way from one of the valves near its left eye and dug into the injury.

Her visor flashed 'Attack Imminent'. With stalking movements, the wolf sniffed a circle around her. She closed her eyes and waited, the beeping of her alarms becoming a metronome in her head.

"Please provide security clearance," the interface said. "Your cooperation is most useful for our data collection."

She opened her eyes. The wolf was staring at her, frustrated and angry. It was stalking up and down in front of her, its eyes boiling.

Why had she been asked to go? Shula was so much better at explaining things, at knowing what to do and say in any situation. The Monarchs had been dead set against it, refusing to even put her name on the team.

"You will be restricted until proper security clearance is provided," the interface said. "Your cooperation is most useful for our data collection."

Hala took a breath and pressed a button on her arm, bringing up the display screen. She scrolled through until she found the codes she had been given.

"Beta-Nine-Z-X security clearance," she said out loud, hoping that the computer could hear her. "Code: four, delta, nine, two …" She looked back at the figures as sweat beaded on her brow. "Foxtrot, three, eight, gamma, five."

The reflection considered her, its pale eyes turning dark and then becoming a deep green. With a jolt, she was knocked off her feet, the powerful paws of the wolf slamming into her chest and pressing her to the ground. Her visor blinked and flashed from screen to screen, frantically calculating chances of escape.

Its teeth were bared, the breath fogging up her helmet, and the iron rods sticking out of its flesh seemed too close. Steam rippled onto her suit and leaked into the fabric; cold shivered on her skin and she wanted to cry.

"Access to the upper levels is

granted," the interface said. "Please proceed."

The wolf looked up as light spilt onto its face, embossing the scars and scabbed tissue in its flesh. Hala breathed hard, despite her suit attempting to normalise her respiration. Fear had taken hold and she felt compelled to heave each breath with all her strength.

But the wolf was transfixed, taking its weight off her and walking towards the light. Hala turned onto her stomach and rose using her arms, legs too shaky to stand. A door had opened at the other end of the corridor, golden light showering onto the floor and walls, silhouetting the wolf.

"Welcome, guest," the interface said, mirroring her awkward position.

"Do you have to do that?" Hala asked, grimacing.

"Mirror interface is designed for comfort and reassurance," the voice said. "People feel less alone when the person they are talking to has the same mannerisms as themselves."

"I find it creepy." She got up, as the wolf vanished into the light. "What's through that door? And what is that wolf thing?"

"The door leads to the main observation lounge," her reflection said.

"I see." She staggered forward. "What about the wolf?"

"No wolves are detected in the area."

"That one that just walked through the door," she waved a hand, and the interface did the same.

"No significant life-forms detected."

"Was anything detected?"

"A swarm of micro-organisms." The interface smiled.

"A swarm …" She rolled her shoulders and stalked forwards. "Is it still in there?"

"It is moving to the upper levels."

"Can you find out what it is? My friend will be very interested to hear about it."

"Please wait."

The interface faded and Hala was left starring at the light oozing from the door ahead. She strained her ears and turned the suit's perceptions to their top setting, but there was no sound of the wolf. The light burned her eyes, so she told the visor to tint. The closer she got to the door, the more her throat felt like it was filled with nettles. Gulping, she stepped through the doorway and onto a moving platform.

Guided upwards and through labyrinthine corridors, Hala felt sick as the floor shivered and shifted. She steadied as doors flew past her and the ceiling became a blur. It went on for minutes that turned into almost an hour. She pulled up the internal memory and searched the legends for any mention of the tower. She found it in the commentary attached to one of the final stories.

> 'We watch the tower, knowing now that the gods will not help. It is not the way. It is how life is; it is how it ought to be. Together we watch as death finds us, and we praise the new gods for their wisdom, for showing us true divinity. We have been blind, believing in the legends that told us what the gods do. We missed the truth. We were so

blind.'

The motion slowed, and a deep red wall loomed at the end of the passage, rearing as the corridor smoothed. The floor stopped and she staggered, only just managing to stay upright. With a gust, the red wall split and opened, leading to a spiral staircase that vanished overhead. She mounted the first step. The whole thing shuddered and screeched into motion, the escalator grinding its gears and pushing her upwards.

At the top of the stairs, she was led onto the roof. The wind pressure made her step back, holding the door frame as she took in her surroundings. Pipes, valves, and old boilers in a spider web of metal. Wind blasted through gaps and howled in hoarse tones.

Hala ducked under a pipe, towards a flickering light. Her breath caught and her heart clenched so tightly that the alarm in her suit went off. Sitting in the centre of a nest of pipes was the wolf. Its eyes found her and its snout flared.

'You will not open the Gate again.'

The message appeared on her visor, stark and prominent. Hala blinked at it and then at the wolf.

'The new god will take you, and you will eat other worlds. We will not allow it.'

"I'm sorry?" She stepped forward,

and the wolf tilted its head.

'The Swarm. We were the gods of this world. Older than any. We are what is left of the people. We were here before humans in their Star Seekers, before they built cities, before they scorched the skies.'

"Why do you look like a wolf?"

The creature stalked closer, its metal limbs and fragmented fur shimmering.

'This was the last living being, the only one with technology we could use. We are the Swarm; we live in the steam. We are the breath of life. We breathed into your suit, and so we speak to you.'

"I'm not trained to do things like

this. Talking to a thing. I mean, a person, or lots of people. I don't …" Her chest fluttered with needles.

'The new god is a true god. It will consume another world. It hungers. It needs to. The craving burns.'

She looked back at the door she had come through. Its mirrored surface showed the interface, but it was stock still. Approaching, she reached out a hand, but the wolf growled at her, a warning sputtering across her visor.

There was smoke in the sky, clouds that boiled, churning with sound that buffeted the suit.

'If you see the face of the sky,

he will make you part of him. You will feed the addiction.' The wolf stalked closer as each word appeared on her visor.

"What do you want from me?" she shouted, anger and fear slicing her in alternating jabs. "I just wanted to make my friend happy. I just wanted to know what was happening."

'We do not care what you wanted. We do not care who you are. The god will use you to escape and feed its habit. The addiction corrodes within it. We must let it starve.'

Hala backed away and clambered onto the rickety pipes that bunched in the centre of the tower. They reached into the clouds.

"Why? What makes you think I'd do something like that? And why didn't you just kill me back in the city? Or downstairs?"

'You are broadcasting your message through the Gate. The other worlds will hear the word of god, and they will fear.'

The ache in her arms came and went as the suit recalibrated her needs. It felt like it took hours to move only a few feet, but she kept at it. Grunting and aching, her suit pumped extra drugs into her blood. Her voice needed to get through to Shula.

'Forget the legends. Forget the myths. They are not the truth of gods.'

The clouds were so close that her visor fogged. Heat was in the pipes, and the suit was struggling to keep her skin from scorching. Pushing through pain and the pull of the wind, she broke into the thick of the storm. There was a clear circle of metal at the top of the great launchpad, a blinking light, and the remains of a skeleton clinging to it.

Hala came close and lifted the head of the dead woman. She saw that she had a gem lodged in her skull over her forehead. It reminded her of Shula and her own gemmed forehead.

She reached the top of the structure and found the blinking light. It was atop a metal pedestal, concealing a set of circuitries. Opening it, she found the atmospheric booster system. The reflection in the metal lid turned into the interface, their expression furious and full of hate.

"You are unauthorised to use this. Stand down."

Hala shook her head. She took the control pad from her suit and redirected the wiring from within it, connecting to the atmospheric software.

"I came here to find out what happened to the planet," she said as she worked. "My job is to report. This is the only option left. I'm sorry if the information is inconvenient for you."

The light blinked faster, and she pressed her control pad, draining power from her breathing tank and pouring it into the processor. It registered and recalibrated. Her breath shortened, cold crept into her skin, and the edges of her sight turned dark. But the clouds were dissipating above, clearing and replaced by a deep, inky sky. Hala smiled as she slipped from her seat and the suit tore from its pipes, ripping away some from her skin. The cold numbed her, but the pressure and strain was making her lose consciousness.

She dangled, unable to move as the connection held her to the top of the structure. With her eyesight failing, she looked up at the sky, hoping to see some sign of what had happened.

Clouds circled and parted, then rose, reforming into a solid shape. As Hala grasped the tower of pipes and her body shuddered into shock, the mist solidified into the shape of a man. He was hunched, his head bowed, and his body was sickly. It was pale fog, creating a pale imitation of humanity.

"Hello?" Hala managed to say. Her visor was telling her everything that was wrong with her suit. She lost track of how many warnings were going off.

"Welcome," said the figure, though his mouth did not move.

Hala gulped her fear. The suit's systems were flickering on and off, unable to regulate her body. It took all her concentration to slow her heart and breathing so that she could think for a moment. The cold, thin air was pushing her in every direction, so she held on tight to the pipes, even as they cut into her and tried to rip her tubes out.

"Are you Cyneric Monarch?" she asked.

"I am God," he replied. "You will be, too, if you but breathe."

"I'd rather not be a god," she choked through a gasp of pain. "And, frankly, looking at this world, you haven't done a very good job of being God."

He lifted his head to make empty eye sockets glower towards her. "What do you know about gods?"

She waited for him to explain. He folded into a cloud of shifting mist, which slowly coalesced into another form, standing this time with long wispy hair.

"If you want to know what makes a god, you need to read more."

"I've been reading," Hala replied, breathless. "Shula made me read mythologies and legends."

"Gods don't work like they do in stories." The fog expanded and contracted with laughter. "If you want to know what makes a god, don't read mythologies, or stories. Read apologetics. Read theologians who wrestle with their gods, and sooner or later, you realise it."

"I read those, too." She struggled to stay in place, each word a wrestle. "Were those your commentaries?"

The fog split into a wave that opened the cloud. It revealed the land below, the desolation, the emptiness. Shells of houses looked like forgotten insect carcasses, and weeds wove scriptures in the sands.

"Gods tend to protect their people." Hala pulled herself up, pain digging into her eyes and back, but she pushed through it. "Gods stop their worlds from dying. If you think you're a god, then you're a god of nothing."

"The world is a testament to how much of a god I am." The voice growled as if taking a rattling breath. "I saw what was happening to this world. I caused much of it, built injustice and suspicion. I thought that would make me a god. I thought that keeping the masses down so that my power would be absolute would raise me above nature. I took the Swarms, the beliefs of the people, and I turned them to my own ways. But that did not make me a god. Anybody can become powerful, anybody can gain influence and control. Read your apologists. The thing that terrifies them most is not the actions of their gods. Quite the opposite.

"To be truly God is subtler. I saw the injustice; I saw the cruelty. I saw fear take hold, and disease chew people up. I saw horrors, and I did what any real god would do. I did nothing."

Hala blinked, unsure if she had heard correctly. "I'm sorry, what?"

"To know that you could change things, that a simple act, a gesture of your power and wealth, would change things for the better, and then to do nothing; that is godhood. Anyone can be powerful. Anyone can be rich. Only a god can feel the rush that comes with letting things burn."

Hala's horror was boiling her. The

suit trembled, its systems rewiring and rerouting. Her ears filled with sound and words flashed warnings all over her cracked visor. She reached out a hand and put it to the pipe nearest to her, hauling her body upright at last. The vision of the man who had made himself a god whirled and became mist, but she could feel the weight of his gaze upon her.

"I can't breathe," she said, pulling on the valves around her neck. This was a wild idea, a horrible plan, something that couldn't possibly work. "Why did you let me come here?" she demanded, panting hard.

"I need to feel it again. That rush! There is no feeling like it. No euphoria that compares. I need to feel it again!"

"Okay," she said. "If you can."

She opened her arms out, and the gasses thundered towards her, burrowing into her oxygen systems. Alarms became too numerous to count. Warning signs plastered the visor until nothing could be seen beyond them. Cloud upon cloud seeped through her lungs and the life support overloaded.

The god put its mind into the computer but found only microchips and wiring. It tried to work, tried to move this way and that. But when the computer would still not let it in, the creature turned its attention on Hala herself. It would plant itself deep into her mind and become her; it would possess her. Then it would walk this husk back through the Gate and into the other world. It would gather all wealth and watch people squabble over what crumbs remained. Truly, then he would be a God among gods.

He opened Hala's eyes, felt the wind rush past her body, just for a moment. He felt gravity pull him down, down, faster and faster.

"Oh," was his final thought before they hit the ground.

About the Author

Joel Cornah is an author, journalist, and blogger. His novels, *The Sea-Stone Sword* and *The Sky Slayer,* were published BFS Award-winning publisher, Grimbold books. He is an editor for *The Science-Fiction and Fantasy Network*, which has featured authors such as Brandon Sanderson and Kameron Hurley, as well as TV stars.

He is outspoken about his dyslexia, supporting efforts to spread awareness through talks, articles, and books.

He runs *The Campaign Trail* podcast, which has featured critically acclaimed authors, such as Anna Smith Spark alongside its regular players.

Also by Joel Cornah

We would like to thank everyone who made this project possible,
via the Kickstarter and outside of it.

Specific thanks goes to:

Aaron Armitage

David Parker

Ross Warren

More dyslexic friendly

titles coming soon...